The LEGEND of SLEEPY HOLLOW

The Legend of Sleepy Hollow

Based on the story by Washington Irving

Retold by *DIANE WOLKSTEIN*
Illustrated by *R. W. ALLEY*

William Morrow and Company, Inc.   New York

Library of Congress Cataloging-in-Publication Data
Wolkstein, Diane.
The legend of Sleepy Hollow.
Summary: A superstitious schoolmaster, in love with a
wealthy farmer's daughter, has a terrifying encounter
with a headless horseman.
[1. Ghosts—Fiction. 2. New York (State)—Fiction]
I. Irving, Washington, 1783–1859. Legend of Sleepy
Hollow. II. Alley, R. W. (Robert W.), ill. III. Title.
PZ7.W8344Le   1987   [Fic]   86-23596
ISBN 0-688-06532-5
ISBN 0-688-06533-3 (lib. bdg.)

To SHIRLEY KELLER, MY FRIEND
~ D.W.

For ZOË
~ R.W.A.

Not far away from the small port of Tarrytown is a little valley among high hills that is one of the quietest places in the world. A small brook glides through it, whose soft murmur lulls those who hear it to want to stop their work and rest. Only the occasional sounds of a woodpecker tapping or a quail whistling disturb the calm of the valley. It is a drowsy, dreamy place, rightly called Sleepy Hollow.

The Dutch people who settled three hundred years ago in this sleepy valley were caught by its bewitching spell and believed in spirits and ghosts. Recently when I went to visit Sleepy Hollow, there was still such a drowsiness in the air that I found my eyes closing as an old woman began to tell me a story. But as she continued, my eyes opened wide in wonder and my heart beat faster, even though I know there are certainly no such things as ghosts. She told me the story of Ichabod Crane and the Headless Horseman....

During the Revolutionary War, a German soldier who was fighting for the British had his head blown off by a cannon. His body was buried in the churchyard. But every evening his ghost would rise from his grave and set out for the battlefield in search of his head. Villagers riding home long after midnight spoke of being struck by a blast of cold air as they approached the church. They said it was from the Headless Horseman hurrying back to his grave before daybreak.

About thirty years after the war, the schoolmaster Ichabod Crane arrived in this remote New York valley that was filled with strange beliefs. He was tall and lank, with narrow shoulders and long arms and legs. His head was small and flat on the top. His ears were huge and his long nose was like a bird's beak. As he walked down the hill to the schoolhouse, with his clothes fluttering about him, he looked like a runaway scarecrow or the hungriest man on earth.

He, too, had his strange beliefs. In fact, although he owned only one suit, two shirts, two neckties, a pair of stockings, one set of underwear, one broken pitch pipe, and one rusty razor, he owned four books: a book of hymns, a book of dreams and fortune-telling, a New England almanac, and a book of witchcraft, from which he was always quoting to the local farmers.

Ichabod lived and ate at the houses of the farmers whose children he taught. At the time this was a necessity for all schoolmasters, since they were paid very little; but it was especially necessary for Ichabod, for though he was thin, he had the eating capacity of a great anaconda snake. To make himself useful and agreeable to the farmers, he helped with the chores. He mended fences, cut hay, took the horses to water, drove the cows to pasture, and cut wood for winter. To please the farmers' wives, he would hold one child on his knee as he rocked the cradle with his other foot.

Still, Ichabod was always hungry and in need of money. To increase his earnings, one evening a week he taught the young people to sing psalms from the Bible. It was at one of these weekly singing lessons that he met the beautiful and wealthy Katrina Van Tassel.

Katrina was a lovely girl, plump, ripe, and as rosy-cheeked as one of her father's peaches. Baltus Van Tassel's barn was as large as a church and brimming with treasures—pigs, geese, ducks, chickens, pigeons, and roosters. When Ichabod entered the Van Tassel farmhouse, filled with pewter, silver, dark mahogany furniture, and every kind of food imaginable, all his thoughts turned to Katrina and how he might win her and the farm for his own. But the task was not so easy, for the beautiful Katrina was a coquette and a flirt, and her feelings changed from day to day.

Before Ichabod began to court Katrina, she had favored a strong country lad named Abraham, or Brom Van Brunt, as the Dutch called him. Nicknamed Brom Bones, he was the hero of the neighborhood. He had broad shoulders, curly black hair, double joints, and a boisterous sense of humor. He and his gang were known to gallop madly past the farmhouses at midnight whooping and shouting, startling the good Dutch housewives from their sleep. When they realized, "Aye, it's only Brom Bones," they would shake their heads in amusement and go back to sleep. They liked Brom's roughness and his good humor.

When Brom Bones saw Katrina turn her fancy to the schoolmaster, he wanted to fight him. But since Ichabod wisely refused to battle, he was forced to play practical jokes instead. By stopping up the chimney, Brom Bones smoked Ichabod and his students out of their singing class. He broke into the schoolhouse at night and turned everything so topsy-turvy that Ichabod was certain that the witches in the neighborhood had chosen his schoolroom for their meetings. But worst of all, he trained a dog to mock Ichabod's singing. When Ichabod serenaded Katrina at twilight with hymns, Brom Bones would set his dog loose nearby. The dog would yowl in the most awful manner—woo–whoooooo———whoo–ooooo—imitating Ichabod's nasal singing.

The spring and the summer of the year went by. Then one fine autumn afternoon when Ichabod sat on his high stool, ruling over his students, a messenger came to the door with an invitation for him to attend a party that evening at the Van Tassels'. Ichabod hurried his pupils through their lessons and dismissed school an hour early.

He rushed to his lodgings at Van Ripper's to prepare himself. He carefully brushed his one rusty black suit. He combed and recombed his hair. He borrowed a horse from Van Ripper so that he might make a good impression on his sweetheart. Gunpowder was a thin, shaggy, broken-down plough horse whose one eye had the gleam of a devil about it.

Gunpowder trotted along and Ichabod scanned the countryside for food. It was a beautiful day. The sky was clear. The trees were brilliant orange, purple, and scarlet. In the bushes, small birds twittered and chirped, frolicking as they ate their last banquet. The trees bore vast stores of red apples. There were long rows of golden Indian corn, under which lay plump orange pumpkins. Ichabod gazed at the fields of buckwheat and changed them in his imagination to well-buttered pancakes that the plump Katrina was heaping upon his plate.

When Ichabod finally arrived at the Van Tassels', the farmhouse yard was already crowded. Farmers and their wives, young men and lasses surrounded Brom Bones, who stood near his trusted horse, Daredevil. Ichabod avoided his rival and went into the parlor of the farmhouse. On the tables there appeared a sight that nearly made his eyes fill with tears: doughnuts, crullers, sweet cakes, shortcakes, ginger cakes, honey cakes, whole families of cakes, followed by apple pies, peach pies, pumpkin pies, slices of ham, smoked beef, roasted chicken, bowls of milk and cream, peaches, pears, plums. Oh, Ichabod's stomach swelled, and his eyes rolled as he chuckled at the thought that one day he would rule over all this luxury.

The music began. As Ichabod danced with his sweetheart, Brom Bones brooded in the corner. When the dancing stopped, Ichabod went onto the porch to listen to war stories, followed by tales of ghosts and spirits. After one villager from Sleepy Hollow finished telling the story of the Headless Horseman, Brom Bones stood up and said, "Just last week, I felt a strong blast of air as I was entering Sleepy Hollow. I was on Daredevil, so I challenged him: 'Come on, first one across the bridge wins a bowl of punch!' The Horseman took up the bet. We raced faster and faster and I was winning, but just as we came to the bridge before the churchyard, the Horseman leapt from his horse and disappeared in a flash of fire."

Then old Brouwer, who didn't believe in ghosts, said, "I wouldn't believe you, Brom, if I hadn't seen him myself. He picked me up one evening from the side of the road and set me down behind him on his horse. Off we rode over hill and swamp until we reached the bridge. Then he turned into a skeleton, and I was thrown into the brook."

Ichabod shuddered at these stories—and yet he loved them. Exchanging ghost stories was his most fearful pleasure. Ichabod contributed some chilling stories of his own that he had read in his book of witchcraft.

Then the party broke up. The farmers gathered together their families and rode home in their wagons. Ichabod stayed to court Katrina. But something must have gone wrong, for when he walked out of the house, his head was down and he looked neither to the left nor to the right of what was to have been his castle. Sadly, he mounted Gunpowder and, with several good kicks, started back to the farm of Van Ripper.

This was an eerie hour of the night to be riding alone with a sad heart. The hush of midnight was in the air. Now and then a rooster crowed or a dog barked, but otherwise there was no sign of life. All the stories of ghosts and goblins that Ichabod had heard that evening came crowding into his mind. The night grew darker. A giant tulip tree with gnarled and twisted limbs loomed up in the dark. Ichabod thought he heard a groan. Two hundred yards from the tree was a small brook that was said to be haunted.

As Ichabod approached the bridge, he kicked Gunpowder as hard as he could in the ribs to go faster. But the old horse turned mean and went sideways instead of straight ahead. He stopped so suddenly he nearly threw Ichabod into the water. Just then Ichabod heard a splash. He looked to the side of the bridge and saw reflected in the water a huge, black shadow.

Ichabod's hair stood straight up. What to do? He gathered his courage and asked, "Who are you?" No answer. He cried louder, "Who are you?" Then the thing moved from the water's edge onto the bridge. It was half horse and half—what? Ichabod did not wait to see but kicked Gunpowder. Gunpowder began to trot. The thing at his side began to trot. Ichabod's heart sank, and he tried to sing a hymn, but he could not open his mouth.

They came to a clearing, and by the light of the moon Ichabod saw with horror that his companion had no head. Then Ichabod's horror turned to terror when he saw that the figure on the horse was carrying his head in front of him on his lap. Ichabod kicked Gunpowder without stopping, and away they dashed. Stones flew and sparks flashed, but the shadowy figure rode just as quickly.

When they reached the crossroad, Ichabod urged
Gunpowder to the right. But Gunpowder, who had
turned as mean as the devil, went left toward the
churchyard. Just then the straps holding Ichabod's
saddle broke, and the saddle slipped to the ground.
Ichabod quickly grabbed on to Gunpowder's tangled
mane, as he heard the huge horse behind him trample
Van Ripper's best saddle. For a moment, Ichabod
feared the farmer's anger, but this was no time for such
fears. Ichabod had all he could do to keep from falling
off his horse.

Just then he saw an opening in the trees, and the
church in the distance. Ichabod thought, "If only I can
reach that bridge, I am safe," for he remembered
Brom's story of the horseman who had disappeared at
that bridge. The other horse was close behind him.
Ichabod kicked Gunpowder, and Gunpowder sprang
across the bridge.

"Safe!" Ichabod thought, and he turned to see if the ghost had disappeared. But at that moment the horseman picked up his head from his lap and threw it with all his strength at Ichabod. The schoolmaster dodged. Too late! It hit his head with a great crash, and he tumbled into the dirt.

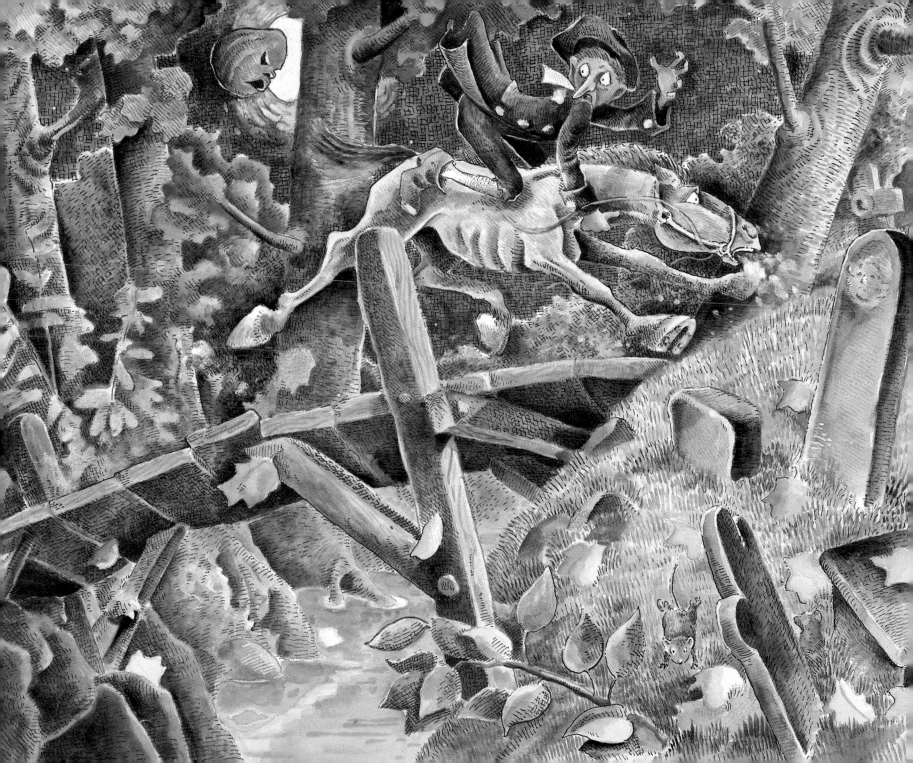

The next morning Gunpowder was found without his saddle at Van Ripper's gate. Ichabod did not appear for breakfast or for dinner. There was no school that day. A search went out to find the schoolmaster. All that was found of Ichabod was his hat on the bank of the brook. Nearby were Van Ripper's saddle and a shattered pumpkin.

Ichabod Crane's body was never found. The next Sunday at church the stories of old Brouwer and Brom Bones were told again. Villagers guessed that Ichabod had been carried off by the Headless Horseman. But an old farmer who visited New York City later said that he had heard that Ichabod was still alive. Heartbroken by Katrina's refusal and afraid of Van Ripper's anger, he had run off to the city to study law and become a well-fed judge.

Meanwhile, Brom Bones married the beautiful Katrina; and whenever he heard the story of Ichabod Crane and the Headless Horseman, he would burst into hearty laughter at the mention of the pumpkin. But whatever Brom knew about the schoolmaster, the old woman who told me the story firmly maintained that it was spirits who took Ichabod Crane away.

Sleepy Hollow is like still water bordering on a rushing stream. Whatever rides in the quiet water turns slowly around and around for a long time. The old schoolhouse is now deserted. But sometimes, a farmer walking home at twilight stops, for, rising from the empty schoolhouse, he thinks he hears Ichabod Crane's nasal voice singing a melancholy hymn. A moment later, a dog starts to whine or to bark....